A New Pony

"Looky, Lucky! Lucky! Lucky!"

"Mmmmm." A very gentle mutter, like a whispered nicker, almost lost in the wind.

I whirl. My feet fly up, and my tail hits ice.

I'm facing into the corner where the old milk parlor joins the barn. Lucky stands like a shadow, deep in the corner. Snow sifts around the corner past Lucky. It lies thinly here, on Mrs. O'Neal's sad daffodils and Lucky's back, and . . . on something on the ground.

Lucky bends her head to it and licks it. She mutters that strange mutter to it.

She wasn't answering me at all. She was talking to . . . to. . . .

It draws long, bony legs up under itself and tries to stand up.

I gasp.

It gets halfway up on its hind legs and collapses.

I say stupidly, "Lucky. You had a baby."

Books by Anne Eliot Crompton

The Rainbow Pony
The Snow Pony
The Wildflower Pony

Available from MINSTREL Books

THE WILDFLOWER PONY

Anne Eliot Crompton

A MINSTREL® BOOK

Published by POCKET BOOKS

New York   London   Toronto   Sydney   Tokyo   Singapore

This book is a work of fiction. Names, characters, places and incidents are products of the author's imagination or are used fictitiously. Any resemblance to actual events or locales or persons, living or dead, is entirely coincidental.

A MINSTREL PAPERBACK *Original*

A Minstrel Book published by
POCKET BOOKS, a division of Simon & Schuster Inc.
1230 Avenue of the Americas, New York, NY 10020

ISBN: 0-671-51120-3

First Minstrel Books printing July 1996

10 9 8 7 6 5 4 3 2 1

A MINSTREL BOOK and colophon are registered trademarks of Simon & Schuster Inc.

Front cover illustration by Michele Manning

Printed in the U.S.A.

This story is for my children:
Carrie, Joseph, Nancy, Catherine, and Samuel;
and for All Readers.

*H*ey, Alice," says Jinny O'Neal on the phone. "There's something funny."

"Affirmative," I agree. "A snow day, April sixth!"

I'm looking out the hall window. You take Niagara Falls and turn it from water to snow, and that's what I'm looking at. The school bus can't get up O'Neal's Hill for Jinny and me. That's okay, it can't go anywhere else, either. School is canceled.

"No." Impatience sharpens Jinny's voice.

"Something funny's happened up here, with us."

"Funny?" I hope she's just calling to tell me a joke; I could use one. And I hope I don't have to pull on coat and boots and gloves and scarf and struggle up to O'Neal Farm through this snowstorm.

"Not funny really," says Jinny. "More like weird."

My heart sinks. "Look, Jinny, just tell me."

"Okay. Lucky's gone—missing."

My heart thumps. "What?"

"You remember Lucky? That little red pony you love like a sister?"

"Come on, Jinny! Tell!"

"Well, actually, she's disappeared."

"Huh? Disappeared?"

The O'Neals' barn has a door like a wall, half as thick as me, with an iron bolt. My Lucky is clever, but she really can't draw that bolt. Besides that, she's in a loose box with Jinny's pony, Jet.

"How could she disappear? Where to?" Out in the whirling snow?

"Search me. Look, Al, I gotta go. We're taking the last of the maple syrup downtown to

Uncle Josh's store. You better get up here, find Lucky, first priority."

"Hey, Jinny—"

Click. Jinny's hung up.

I hang up and stare out the window.

My Lucky Pony lives in the O'Neals' barn with Jinny's black Jet Pony, and Cow, and Jack's chickens, and Jerry's rabbits, and Jan's orphan coon, and the barn cats. I pay Lucky's room and board by helping with chores. Once a day I climb the steep dirt road to shovel manure, measure out feed, gather eggs, and brush Lucky.

Today I meant to wait till after the storm. But if Lucky's really missing . . . Lucky? MISSING?

"Grandma! Grandma!"

Grandma doesn't answer. She's pretty deaf.

I find her at the kitchen table. Sorting old rags to cut for her new quilt, she hums a hymn. I think it's the one that says, "O God who gives the winter's cold/As well as summer's joyous ray . . ." Jinx, the tricolored cat Jan O'Neal gave her, lies curled in the rag pile. Lately Jinx has got fat and slow. But she looks up as I lean and touch Grandma's shoulder.

Grandma gives a little jump. "Alice? Why aren't you in school?" Between humming and sorting, Grandma's forgotten what's happening.

"Snow day, Grandma." I say it loudly and point to the window, where snow whirls past Grandma's embroidered curtains.

"Oh. Snow day. I forgot!" Grandma takes off her glasses to rest her eyes. "It's just sugar snow, Alice. Spring snow, like you pour maple syrup on at a sugar-off. You going up to O'Neal's to chore?"

I nod. No use worrying Grandma about Lucky, at least till I know what's happened.

"I'll fix pot pie for lunch." Grandma means, be home in time for it.

Minutes later, bundled in sweater, coat, boots, scarf, and mittens, I wade up the road. I lean into the snowy wind. There's ice under the snow. That stopped the school bus but not Mr. O'Neal. His pickup has a snowplow on it. He and Jinny must have just driven downtown with the last of the maple syrup. Their tire tracks slide and veer all over the road. I slip in them. Twice, I fall down.

There's O'Neal's farmhouse like a huge shadow behind blowing snow.

4

I follow the drive around to the barn, still stumbling in the pickup's tracks.

I draw the great iron bolt and step out of windy snow into dim warmth. Safe at last! I draw the door shut behind me.

Chickens cluck and scratch in the straw. Kittens play. Lying in her stanchion, Cow swings her head toward me. Jet whinnies from the big box stall he shares with Lucky.

There's no sound from Lucky. Not a stamp, not a whicker.

Breathing in the sweet hay-smell, I pass Cow and the big rabbit hutches and lean on the box stall. Right off, I see the stall door has been kicked out. That's how Lucky got out of the stall. Some O'Neal mended the door with baling wire right away.

Jet nods at me and mutters. His kind, dark eyes shine at me. He's a big black pony, almost as big as a horse. He's maybe fifteen years old. Jan's orphan coon, Ring, sits curled on his broad back.

I look carefully all around the barn.

There are hay bales, straw bales, feed tins. Rakes, hoes, shovels, spades. Cow, chickens, cats, rabbits. No Lucky.

Where can Lucky have gone? How? Why?

Why would any creature—especially my bright Lucky—want to go out in the sugar-snow storm?

Lately Lucky hasn't been so bright.

I got Lucky through a sort of miracle last summer. She was on a truck that turned over. The driver didn't know what to do with her so he gave her to me.

Jinny was there. Jinny and Jet helped Lucky and me till we got used to each other. Lucky lives up here because I don't have a barn or company for her.

Last summer Lucky was lively and fun. After some grazing and grooming she even turned pretty, with her white-tipped red coat all glossy, and her white mane and tail floating soft.

But over the long winter in the loose box she's gotten fat. Maybe even dull. I didn't want to think it before, but it's true. My fat, winter-coated Lucky has turned dull.

Today should be spring. Lucky should be galloping with Jet in Back Field right now. Jinny says she'll come back to her old self after a few good gallops.

I call, "Lucky? Looky, Lucky?"

Jet blows softly and paws the sawdust bedding. He would tell me the story if he could.

I search the barn.

I search behind hay bales and feed bins and in among hanging tack and tools. There's the hayloft. I look up the ladder. Then I tell myself, Don't be a coconut! Lucky can't climb that ladder. Leastwise, not while she's so fat.

There's the old milk parlor. Nowadays it's mostly used for storing odds and ends that might be useful sometime, somehow. The door leans open. Cobwebs in the doorway hang broken.

I push through, in among broken chairs, leaky pots, coils of rope, threadbare rugs, and the old manure spreader Mrs. O'Neal hopes to sell as an antique.

"Lucky? Looky, Lucky!"

Sighing wind answers me, and a rush of cold air.

There in the corner, two boards have been punched out. Kicked out. Snow whirls in through the new hole. Jinny was in a hurry to go with her dad. She didn't get to follow Lucky's trail this far.

I open the door. Snow rattles in my face. Here I am, out in the storm again, wobbling on ice again.

"Looky, Lucky! Lucky! Lucky!"

"Mmmmmm."

"Lucky?"

"Mmmmmm." A very gentle mutter, like a whispered nicker almost lost in the wind.

I whirl. My feet fly up, and my tail hits ice.

I'm facing into the corner where the old milk parlor joins the barn. Lucky stands like a shadow, deep in the corner. Snow sifts around the corner past Lucky. It lies thinly here, on Mrs. O'Neal's sad daffodils and Lucky's back, and . . . on something on the ground.

Lucky bends her head to it and licks it. She mutters that strange mutter to it.

She wasn't answering me at all. She was talking to . . . to . . .

It draws long, bony legs up under itself and tries to stand up.

I gasp.

It's small and thin. Red like Lucky but a gentler, paler red. Its mane and tail are like tufts of cotton, stuck on.

Wide, seeing eyes look out of its face. It sees

the blowing snow, and big, warm Lucky leaning down, and me staring it in the face.

It gets halfway up on its hind legs and collapses.

I say stupidly, "Lucky. You had a baby."

"Mmmmm." Lucky breathes warmth on him.

Now, why in the cosmos didn't I see that? I thought my Lucky was fat! Well, she's thin again now! Got her girlish figure back. I thought she was dull! And all the while she was making, sheltering this wonderful baby. This tiny foal who sees and breathes and moves. This living bundle of blood and bone and sinew and horse sense. I know he's got horse sense inside his brand-new head right now. He sees and hears right now the way a horse sees and hears.

He's a miracle.

Holy cosmos! Why didn't I guess?

April 6
11 A.M.

*L*ater, in the barn, Jinny stares. Her blue eyes fairly pop.

She stands almost still, except her thin hands grab air the way she would like to grab the foal. I've never seen her too excited to talk before. Jinny can deal with anything. Jinny's got a word for everything. Nothing gets to Jinny. Till now.

I say, "His name's Sugar. For sugar snow."

Jinny nods. Gulps. Shakes snow from her long red hair.

Sugar leans against Lucky, safe in the loose box. He stands pretty well already. When he wobbles, she bends and licks him. His red coat and cotton mane and tail have dried all curly. Jet's loose out here with us. He hangs his head over the door and watches Sugar with a kind, sort of fatherly interest.

Jinny swallows and blinks. Finally she croaks, "Cosmic."

"Affirmative," I agree.

"I never guessed."

"Me neither."

"You know something, Al. I think Jan knew. He spent a lot of time around this loose box."

Jinny's little brother, Jan, doesn't know much. Jinny says he's "not too bright," and that's a nice way of putting it. He's eight years old and would be in second grade if he went to school. He can't count well enough to play cards. But he does have his own special gift, which makes him very useful on O'Neal Farm. He talks to animals. You could say animals talk to him.

I tell Jinny, "Jan did know. He came out and found us in the snow."

This morning Jan did not seem surprised. He

walked past me where I sat in the snow and right up to Lucky. He walked with aim and purpose, not wandering as he usually does. He crouched beside Sugar.

Lucky tossed her head and stamped snow. She was not too happy being bothered right then. She might have bitten anybody else but Jan and me.

Jan paid her no attention. He touched the wet, shivery foal and crooned to him, the way he croons to his pet coon.

Lucky laid her ears way back.

Still weak with surprise, I quavered, "Jan. Jan, I wouldn't touch him just yet. Lucky doesn't like it."

Jan paid no attention to me.

Sugar gathered his long legs and reared his front end.

Jan grabbed him.

His little, thin arms went around the foal's chest and rump. Jan staggered to his feet, bringing the foal up with him. The foal was nearly Jan's size, but Jan actually lifted him up in his arms and carried him.

"Hey!" I scrambled up, slipped, fell down, and rose again, just like Sugar. "Hey, wait."

Jan paid no attention. He turned around, the foal clasped against him, and made for the milk parlor door I had left open.

Lucky followed close on his heels, licking the foal over his shoulder.

I followed Lucky.

Jan led us into the snowless, windless barn, and all the way to the loose box.

In the loose box Jet whinnied joyfully and stretched his head far over the half-wall to greet the foal.

I panted. "Wait . . ." Now I guessed that this was why Lucky had run out in the snow to have her baby. She didn't want Jet's big hoofs trampling him by mistake. The snow seemed safer to her than the loose box.

Jan paid no attention. He set Sugar on his brand-new feet. Sugar wavered till Lucky licked him. Then he keeled over.

Jan opened the loose box door. He took hold of Jet's halter and let him out of the loose box.

I said, "Wait! Let me."

Together, Jan and I lifted the foal up again and into the loose box. Lucky followed, trampling our heels, breathing warm air down our frozen necks. Jan and I came out together and closed the door. Lucky and the foal stayed inside. Jet stayed loose outside, with us. He still stands here now, with Jinny and me, watching the foal.

Absently, eyes on Sugar, Jinny pats Jet's nose. "You'd think it was his foal." More sharply she adds, "I bet he thinks it is!"

We both know that can't be. Jet is a gelding; he can't be a father.

I rewind my memories. "Lucky must have been bred before that day when we got her from the wreck."

Jinny nods.

"And if we hadn't got her she would have been dog meat, remember?"

Jinny nods.

"And so would he! He would never have been born."

"Affirmative."

We lean on the door and watch Sugar.

Carefully he turns himself around and finds Lucky's udder. His little cotton tail wags as he sucks. Lucky licks his bony rump.

Jinny asks me, "Al, what did you do for Lucky this morning? After he was born?"

"Nothing. I didn't know what to do, and she

seemed okay." She's fine! Now I remember. "Jan brought her some feed." Then Jan went off and disappeared like a shadow, the way he does.

We don't usually give the ponies feed; it makes them too lively. But I could see this was a first priority occasion.

"What did you do for the birth cord?"

"Nothing." It still dangles from Sugar's lean belly.

Jinny says, "You can cut it, but most likely it will dry up by itself. What about the . . . the . . . afterbirth?"

"The what?"

"You didn't see anything out there in the snow? Any mess?"

"Negative."

"I bet Lucky ate it."

"Ick!"

Jinny says wisely, "They do that so wolves won't smell it and come after the baby."

"How do you know all this?"

"Cow has a calf every spring, you know. And the rabbits . . . Well, at least Lucky got some feed. Good thing we've got Jan around here, isn't it."

"Jan's smarter than everybody thinks, Jinny."

"He's smart with animals."

"He's nice, too."

Jinny nods. Then she asks, "Al. What's your folks going to say to this?"

"Holy Honolulu!" All this time I haven't given my folks a thought. Now it hits me.

"Your dad wasn't crazy about you having Lucky, all by herself."

"No kidding!"

"What'll he think of you having two of them?"

"Blastoff, Jinny! I don't know!"

Lucky gets tired of nursing Sugar. She swishes her tail and pushes him away. He drops into the sawdust and stretches out flat. Lucky paws sawdust into a bed and plunks herself down beside him.

Two of them. I've got two of them now to take care of.

For a second I feel Sugar Baby heavy on my heart. Jan must have felt him a heavy burden to carry. So will I! Now I will have to make sure that Sugar, like Lucky, has shelter and hay and exercise. I will have to brush him, too, and watch out he doesn't get worms or grubs, and douse him with medicine if he does. Wintertime, I'll have to shovel his manure out of the loose box. The thought sweeps over me like a dark snow-cloud.

But then spring and sun shine again in my heart.

After I got Lucky last year a sort of rainbow grew inside me. I felt as if I shone inside. As I grew stronger and happier, the rainbow grew brighter. Now I'm feeling that rainbow again.

"About my dad," I tell Jinny. "I'll have to break it to him gently. Slowly."

"Not right away."

"Maybe not for ages."

That reminds me, Grandma said something about pot pie for lunch.

"I've got to go," I tell Jinny. I'm starved! But still I hang over the loose box door. I can't take my eyes off my ponies.

"You going to tell your Grandma?"

"Blastoff, I can't!" This is going to be one hard secret to keep! "I wish I could tell her." She'd be as excited as I am.

"Lucky," I say, "I'll be back."

Lucky mutters to Sugar.

"I'll be back before you know I've gone."

I won't be able to stay away.

May 1
11 A.M.

*H*arry Barns says, "Well, my rotted socks!"

He sits in the tree house door, staring down at us. I sit on Lucky, grinning up at him. This is our first tree house meeting this year.

This morning I saw a blue scarf tied to the big apple tree beside O'Neal Road. That's our signal to meet in our secret tree house.

I wasn't sure Sugar could make it this far. This would be his first trip farther than the orchard. But I figured we would try.

I finished my chores early. Jinny was just commencing her chores when I bridled Lucky.

"Don't take it wrong," I told her, "but I'm going out alone for a while."

To my surprise, Jinny just said, "Okay." I figured she had something else on her mind.

Sugar trotted briskly beside Lucky all the way through Blueberry Lot and across Old Pasture and up Rocky Rise. We rested up there awhile, looking down on my house and farther down on Granton, Massachusetts, and way on down to Granton Tire and Tube, where Dad works. I turned and watched my back trail.

When I knew no one had followed, I guided Lucky back down the Rise and across Old Pasture, straight to the secret tree house.

Now Harry points. "What's that?"

Sugar glows in the May sunshine. His soft red coat shows white freckles. His little tail floats like dandelion fluff. But his long legs tremble after this trip, and his head hangs.

I laugh up at Harry. "What do you think?"

"Did you know about it?"

"Never guessed! I just thought Lucky was fat."

Lucky nods and paws the stony ground. She

knows that here at the tree house, she gets turned loose to graze.

I slide down, take off her bridle, and hang it from a maple branch.

Sugar shies away from me. The horse sense born in him warns him about me. I'm a human alien. He still doesn't like me too close.

Lucky swishes her white tail and goes for the new grass. Sugar copies her, nosing the grass. Once in a while he actually eats a wisp.

I climb the rope ladder. Harry scrunches sideways. We sit together in the doorway, legs dangling in the air.

We've seen each other in school all year, but from far off. At school we pretend we barely know each other. Even Jinny doesn't know what really good friends we are. This way we don't get a bunch of dumb comments we don't need.

Harry says, "This sure is a crunch!" It was tight last year, both of us in the tree house. But not like this.

"You know what, Harry? We've grown."

"Bingo."

We've grown, all right. Harry is taller and a bit heavier than last year. His brown hair was neat before. Now it shines like Lucky's coat, as though it's been groomed. But his brown eyes are just as warm as last year.

I wonder if he thinks I've changed.

Sugar folds himself down in Lucky's shade.

"He's tired," Harry says in my ear.

"Sure is. This is the farthest he's ever come from Back Field."

"What's his name?"

"Sugar. He was born in that sugar-snow storm in April."

"Your dad know?"

"No. I don't dare tell him. He'll think I can't take care of Sugar."

"You take care of Lucky just fine."

"I hope Dad sees it like that." But I worry that he won't.

"Your grandma know?"

"No. I can't tell her, she'd think Dad should know." And that hurts. I would love to share Sugar with Grandma!

Sugar stretches out in Lucky's shade. He flicks his cotton tail once, and sleeps.

Harry asks, "Which horse do you like best?"

I look down thoughtfully on Lucky's glossy red back where I love to sit, and on Sugar's soft red fuzz, almost lost in dandelions. Actually, I love both ponies too much. Jinny says ponies are livestock, not pets. All the same, I notice she cares more about old Jet than she lets on.

I say coolly, "I guess I really like Lucky best, because I've had her for a year. But I've got a sort of coconut for Sugar, too."

"I just bet! If I had a dog . . ."

"You want a dog, Harry?"

Harry sighs. "So bad it hurts."

"I bet!" I know that hurting want. I wanted a pony that way, back before Lucky.

"If I had a dog, right now I'd be teaching him tricks for the circus."

Huh? "What circus?"

Harry turns toward me. "Don't you know about the animal act?"

"What animal act?"

"Batman, Al! The Fourth of July?"

"What Fourth of July?"

We laugh.

Granton, Massachusetts, wakes up on the Fourth of July, Independence Day. There's always a parade down Main Street, with the high school band and the Veterans' band, and floats, and kids in costumes, and politicians with signs saying, Vote for Me.

"They don't have an animal act." Never mind a circus!

"They do this year, with all sorts of animals. All sorts of tricks. For five hundred dollars."

What! "There's a five-hundred-dollar prize?"

"What I said. Five hundred dollars."

"Five hundred . . . Look, Harry, that just can't be true. They've never had a prize that big." The biggest prize I ever saw was one hundred for the oldest antique shiny car that still drove.

"Well, they're having it now. Something to do with Granton Alive." That's the first priority push that's on to bring more business and money to town.

"Five hundred dollars. That's cosmic." Absolutely cosmic.

"If I had a dog . . ."

Gloomily, we stare down from our tree house at Lucky and Sugar out in the sunshine. Lucky shakes her mane and blows. Sugar opens his eyes.

I think out loud. "Maybe Jan O'Neal knows how to teach a pony tricks."

"You mean Jan O'Neal the Reject?"

I surprise myself at how mad that makes me. "Jan's not a reject, Harry Barns!"

"Well. He's not very swift."

"Okay, he's not swift with stuff like talking and computers and such."

"Over and out."

"But you show Jan O'Neal any animal, wild or tame, he talks to it. It talks to him. I didn't know Sugar was going to be born, but Jan knew."

"Rotted socks."

"So I don't want to hear you call him a reject anymore."

"Okay, Al. Truce."

Our eyes meet. We laugh.

Harry says, "You ask your pal Jan how to teach Lucky a trick. She could win with just an easy trick because he, the foal, is cute."

Sugar lurches up, lean hind end first, and makes for Lucky's udder. She mutters and licks him. She stands quiet for a moment while his cotton tail swings and jerks with delight. For a moment, Sugar drinks his fill. Then Lucky moves on, after the next grass blade.

"Actually," Harry says, "I know somebody who's programming a horse right now. But she'd never tell you how."

"Who's that?"

"Name's Rowan Rich. Goes to private school. She's got this gorgeous white Arabian horse she calls Shah. And she's teaching him some kind of trick for this circus."

"Hah." If this Rowan Rich can teach a horse, Jinny and I should be able to. I decide. "Harry, I think you're right. Lucky could win." In my mind I hear a crowd cooing, Isn't he CUTE! Isn't the mare PRETTY! And smart, too. They're worth five hundred dollars just to look at them!

"I'll see what Jan knows about programming horses." Thing is, how do I ask Jan anything? Jan doesn't talk to people.

Now, Dad might know. Only Dad mustn't find out about Sugar.

"Hey! I just thought! My dad can meet Sugar at the circus!"

Harry looks questions at me.

I explain. "See, I train these ponies. They sign up for the circus. That means they're in the July Fourth parade."

"Bingo."

"And that's where my dad sees Sugar first time. In the parade!"

"Yeah." Harry brightens.

"Sugar will look so good . . . Dad will be so proud . . ."

Harry nods. "Blastoff."

"And then when Sugar wins the circus— Harry, I gotta go." Already I'm swinging down the rope ladder. "I gotta talk to Jan O'Neal!"

"Okay." Harry leans out the door after me. "But watch for our signal, Al."

"You watch, too. I might signal you!"

May 1
2 P.M.

*J*inny! There's a prize of five hundred dollars for an animal act, July Fourth!"

"I knew that."

We've got Lucky and Jet tied to the back field fence and we're brushing them down. They still have a bit of heavy winter hair mixed with their sleek, new summer coats. Our stiff brushes pull out the extra fluff and send it flying.

Sugar lies resting, folded down in a bed of white bluetts.

"You knew that? Why didn't you say?"

Jinny shrugs. "I was thinking about it this morning." So that's what she had on her mind this morning! "But how are we going to program these dumb ponies for tricks? Now, if anybody had a dog . . ."

"Let's ask Jan how to teach them."

"Hah!" Jinny's brush goes back to work. Happy Jet stamps and swishes his tail. "You can forget about asking Jan. "

I think of silent Jan's quiet, blank face and know what Jinny means.

She unties Jet and slaps his rump. "Go on, boy." Jet shakes mane, swishes tail, and trots off to graze. "So what do you have in mind, Al?"

I brush down Lucky's newly slim side. "Five hundred dollars is an awful lot of money."

"Bingo!"

"I could keep Lucky and Sugar forever on that."

"Negative."

"Huh?" I pause to pull Lucky's long, white-tipped red hairs out of the brush.

"Make that two hundred fifty dollars. I'm in this, too, you know."

"Okay. Two hundred fifty would go a long way to keep Lucky and Sugar. Honolulu, I bet I could buy a saddle!" And not have to scramble up and down Lucky, or bounce to her trot.

I pat Lucky's glossy neck and turn her loose. She prances off toward Jet.

In a flash, little Sugar is up and rocking after her on legs that look too long.

"So what trick would we do, Al?"

I think about the TV circus I saw. "We could dress up in bathing suits with ruffles and stand on the ponies' backs. Then they canter round and round." And the band plays.

I think again. "Or we could train Jan's Ring Coon to ride round and round . . ."

"And jump from Lucky to Jet and back . . ."

"Or the barn cats could ride, sixteen of them at a time. . . . Ponies juggling cats . . ."

"Or we could jump on and off and turn cartwheels . . ."

"Or we could turn cartwheels on their backs, cantering around . . . Hey, there's lots of tricks!"

We laugh together.

I tell Jinny, "Harry Barns thinks the ponies could win just because of Sugar." Uh-oh! Will Jinny catch on that I've been seeing Harry?

She doesn't seem to notice. "You mean, because he's so cute? I think your Harry's all wet."

"Jinny, he isn't MY Harry!"

"More yours than mine. You were the one went and made a truce. Say, Al. Did I just say we should have a dog? Look."

Far on the other side of Back Field, where the old fence disappears among wild rose-bushes, stands a black sort-of wolf.

"Blast off! It's as if you called him, Jinny."

"Well"—Jinny shakes her head—"I was thinking of a handsomer dog."

From here I can't see the dog that well. He's just a big black shadow on the edge of Blue-berry Lot.

"You've seen him before?" I ask Jinny.

"Affirmative. He's been around. He's pretty ugly. Watch, now."

Dog has been studying our ponies in the mid-dle of Back Field. Now he limps toward them slowly, one paw at a time.

"He's been hurt." I notice sympathetically.

"Maybe by a car."

Dog limps steadily, slowly, forward. Now I can see his matted, rusty black coat, his missing ear, his half-tail. The poor thing is a disaster area. His eyes are fixed on . . .

"Jinny! He's hunting Sugar!"

The three ponies bunch together, watching Dog. Sugar hides behind Lucky.

"Don't worry, Al. Keep watching."

Dog sits down in the short grass. He looks away and around, as though he had nothing special on his mind.

Lucky turns half away and snatches a blade of grass. Sugar peeps at Dog around her tail. Then he turns away, too.

Jet stands his ground, head high, ears forward.

Dog lowers his front half to the ground. Inch by inch, he creeps forward. I can see his hard, hunter's eyes still focused on Sugar.

"Jinny . . ."

"It's okay. You'll see."

Jet stretches his head forward and bugles a warning.

Dog stops his crawl.

Dog and Jet make eye contact.

Dog commences to crawl forward once more.

Jet neighs, paws earth, shakes mane.

Dog freezes, close to earth as a snake.

Jet launches himself at Dog.

"There," Jinny says proudly. "You see? Not to worry."

Dog leaps, whirls, runs.

But he limps. Jet thunders down on him. Dog dodges. Jet catches up with him and arches down to bite. But Dog doubles back and around and vanishes through the broken-down fence by Blueberry Lot.

Jet trots up and down by the fence, shrilling and tossing his mane.

Jinny sighs happily. "That was good. Better than TV."

"Jinny," I remind her, "that's my Sugar Baby out there. How long has this . . . monster . . . this Danger Dog, been after him?"

"Couple days. It's okay, Al. Jet takes care of Sugar like he's his daddy."

Jet trots back to Lucky and Sugar. The three ponies swing tails and nuzzle.

"I'm putting my ponies back in the barn at night!"

Jinny shrugs. "Suit yourself. Extra work for you."

"How about Jan? Has he seen this Danger Dog?"

"Must have. But I don't think even Jan could do much with that dog. He's wild."

Maybe not. But someone needs to do something before poor Danger Dog either eats my Sugar Baby or starves.

"Trust old Jet, Al. Sugar's safe with him."

Old Jet's good, all right. But my Sugar's coming in at night.

* * * * * * * * * * * * * **5**

May 10
5 P.M.

My heavens!" Grandma cries. "Oh, my goodness me! Oh, mercy!"

I drop the pan I'm scrubbing back into the sink and run to her in the living room. "What is it, Grandma?"

Grandma came in here a moment ago to fetch her big scrap basket. She needed some bits for the quilt spread on the kitchen.

Now she sits on the window seat, looking into the basket. Her rose-embroidered curtains

34

drape down around her. Beyond, rain drums the bow window.

"What is it, Grandma? You okay?" I lean in the door. The scrubber in my hand drips on the floor.

"Sweeties!" she cooes.

Is she talking to me?

"What charmers!" she murmurs to the basket.

"Grandma?" I'm getting worried. Maybe she hit her head.

"Alice, dear, come look!"

Okay. I walk over to the window seat, drip-drip, and poke my nose into the big scrap basket.

On and under the bright soft cloth scraps tiny fur scraps wiggle. They have big heads and tiny tails. My first thought is, mice! But these are all different colors.

Three fur scraps are black and white. There's a yellow one, a tiny black one, and two tricolor ones like Jinx Cat.

"Oh," I say. "Oh, Honolulu!" I sit down, scrubber and all.

The kittens' eyes are squeezed shut, but they can hear. At the sound of our voices they wiggle and squeak. Jinx Cat bounds up on the window seat between us. She pokes her head in the basket and paws her kittens. Some she licks, and some she rearranges. The kittens squirm and squeal.

I look up at Grandma. "What's Dad going to say?"

"Land of Goshen! That's what I'm wondering myself."

Dad has been very nice about Jinx Cat, whom he didn't want in the first place. Jan O'Neal gave her to Grandma. Now that Grandma sells embroidery to a store down in Granton, she can afford to buy cat food, for Jinx.

"So many of them, Grandma." I'm counting off cans of cat food per day.

"Right now Jinx feeds them. See?" Jinx settles down in the basket and pulls the kittens in to nurse. Each kitten gets a teat except the tiny black one. Nursing, the kittens fall silent. Except the tiny black one, who still squeaks.

Grandma says hopefully, "I'll have time to find them new homes later."

"Hmmm." I know from O'Neals' barn cats,

it's not always that easy to find homes for kittens.

"They'll be cute," Grandma assures me. "They'll be adorable."

Her wrinkled face shines softly as she looks at her kittens. Her skinny, veined hands touch them softly, one by one. I know what she feels.

I think of little Sugar. I see him skipping about Back Field, knee-deep in dandelions. Right now I guess he's standing between Lucky and Jet under the tin rain shelter.

My secret spills out of me. "You know something, Grandma? I've got a baby, too."

"Eh? What say?" Grandma lifts suddenly sharp gray eyes to me.

"I said . . ." Do I really want to say this?

"What, Alice?"

"I . . . I've got a baby, too."

"What!"

"I mean, Lucky has a baby. A foal. His name is Sugar."

Grandma watches and hears me say this. Her jaw drops. For a moment her eyes go sort of woozy.

"A foal, you say. Lucky has a foal."

Eyes on Jinx and her kittens, I tell and sign Grandma the story of my sugar-snow pony.

"Well!" she breathes. "My heavens!"

"You can't tell Dad, Grandma!"

Grandma shrugs. "He'll have to know, dear."

"I've got it all set. Dad will meet Sugar at the circus."

"What say? Circus, did you say?"

I tell Grandma about the circus and the prize Sugar will win. "Then, after he's won, Dad will like him."

Grandma looks at me doubtfully. I doubt that she can find these kittens homes. She doubts that Dad will appreciate Sugar.

The front screen door slams shut. Dad's footsteps come down the hall. He's home early from Tire and Tube.

Grandma doesn't hear these sounds.

Right quick, I snatch an embroidered pillow from the window seat and toss it over the basket, cats and all. I call, "Dad," jump up, and run out in the hall.

He's making for the kitchen and the smell of Irish stew. My excitement startles him. He's used to me being shy with him. He almost smiles at me.

He looks into the living room and says, "Hi, Mom."

Grandma hurries toward him, blocking his view of the window seat. "Irish stew tonight," she says, and tiptoes to kiss his cheek.

He frowns. "What's that noise?" Back in the covered basket the hungry black kitten is mewling.

Quickly I say, "Maybe there's a cat outside wants in."

"Oh. Well, be sure you don't let him in. One cat's enough around here."

Grandma says, "Come on out to the porch. Alice has some news for us. Alice, tell about the circus."

In moments, Dad is stretched in his hammock on the back porch, beer in hand, watching rain drip from the roof. Back in the house, past the smell of Irish stew, Grandma is hiding the scraps basket full of cats. I sit in the garden chair by Dad and tell him all about the circus. He really seems interested.

"Five hundred dollars!" he marvels, same as I did. "That would sure beat babysitting down at Taylors'. So what are you planning on, Al? Your pony and Jane's don't do tricks."

"They don't right now. But we're going to teach them."

Dad chuckles. "You and Jane are going to train two adult ponies by July Fourth?"

"Jinny, Dad. Her name's Jinny."

Dad takes a swig. "I never can remember that name. You figured out how to do it?"

I give Dad my most appealing smile. "I was figuring I'd ask you how."

If anyone besides Jan O'Neal knows how to program a pony for a trick, it's Dad. He doesn't like being responsible for animals, but he knows all about them. Dad's told me everything I know about birds and fireflies and weasels and rabbits and snakes and ants. He likes to tell me about things like that.

But does he want to talk at all right now? I watch him carefully.

First he takes another swig. Wipes his mouth on his sleeve. Looks away over my shoulder into the falling rain.

Then he says, "What you've got to remember, Al. Animals are creatures of habit."

"Right." I lean forward eagerly, smile like I'm selling toothpaste.

"You want to begin the way you want to go

on. It's too bad your ponies are so old. If you'd commenced when they were foals . . ."

"How early can you start training a foal?"

"Oh, glory! First priority, you halter him. Month old, six weeks. Then you can handle him."

Halter! It's past time already Sugar had a halter!

"You can't put any weight on him till he's well grown. But you can lead him around, get him used to taking orders . . . Hey, why are we talking about foals? You and Jenny have got grown animals, here.

"Well. First thing I'd do, I'd take my Taylor baby-sitting money and buy a tape recorder."

"What?"

Swig. Wipe. "Animals are creatures of habit. Yours are in the habit of quiet. Wide-open space. Birds singing. I bet the sound of their own hoofs on pavement will scare them, come the Fourth. Even without horseshoes."

I hadn't thought of that! Dad is so right. Our ponies have never needed shoes. Their hoofs hardly ever touch hard pavement, they just pound earth. And now I remember, riding down to baby-sit at Taylors', the sound of their

41

bare hoofs on that little bit of pavement startles them.

Dad says, "Never mind the crowd . . . the band blaring—off-key."

Over and out!

"So I would buy a tape recorder and play it to my ponies every time I rode. And while I brushed them. All the time."

Harry has a tape recorder I can borrow.

"What kind of tape, Dad?"

"Why, band music! John Philip Sousa!"

Affirmative. Definitely, affirmative.

"And I would ride them down into Granton now and then, let them see cars and people."

Yes!

Dad asks, "What kind of trick do you have in mind?"

"Oh . . . we were thinking of sort of a dance routine."

Grandma pokes her head out the kitchen door. "Alice, how would you and Jinny like circus costumes?"

"Circus costumes! Grandma, we'd win for sure!"

"Well, I don't think you'd win without. You

need to dress the part, you know. You and Jinny are the same size, aren't you?"

"She's skinnier." I show "skinnier" with my hands.

"No problem," Grandma says grandly. "I found some real nice pieces in the basket underneath— Hmmm. I'll get right on it."

She ducks back into the kitchen. The smell of Irish stew strengthens. Grandma hums triumphantly, "Crown Him With Many Crowns."

I sit here, stunned. I can see me and Jinny in shiny satin, Lucky and Jet doing a dance routine, and Sugar with daisies in his halter, stealing the crowd's heart.

We are going to win the five hundred dollars! Holy Honolulu, we are going to win!

"Dance routine," says Dad, staring at the rain. "Now, first priority . . ."

And in the time it takes Grandma to cook dumplings he tells me just how to train the ponies.

We are going to win this five hundred dollars! Jinny and I and Lucky and Jet and especially Sugar are going to win! The five hundred dollars are in our bags right now.

6

Harry and I sit squashed together in the tree house, cool among rustling maple leaves. Out in the sun Lucky grazes. Sugar bounds around her, stiff-legged. His cotton mane and tail bounce with each bound. The silly dandelion chain around his neck swings and shines.

Harry asks, "Who gave him dandelions?"

"Me, of course."

"Come on, Al!"

Our eyes meet. We grin. Harry knows me

too well to think I would do something child-ish like that.

"Actually, I don't know. Someone puts flowers on him when I'm not looking." And I leave them there. Why not?

Thoughtfully, Harry asks, "Will Sugar come if you call him?"

"No, he won't. He won't even come when Lucky calls him."

"You'd better start training him, Al. At the rate he's growing, pretty soon he'll be too strong for you to train. He'll leave you in his dust."

"You think he's growing?"

"Bigger every time I see him."

"I haven't noticed."

"That's because you see him every day. Same thing with my cousin's baby. Grows right in front of you, and my cousin doesn't notice."

"Actually, I'm getting a halter for Sugar."

"Can't you make one out of rope?"

"Not soft and smooth enough for that baby face."

"How about cutting down an old halter?"

"The old O'Neal halters are rotted, bad as your socks."

"Oh, my rotted socks!" We laugh. "What did you want me for, Al?" This time, I was the one who left the blue scarf signal tied to the apple branch.

"Two things. First priority, Will you lend me your tape recorder?"

"Hey! That's my jewel in my crown! What for?"

"To train the ponies for the circus. It's my dad's idea." I explain how the ponies need noise to program them for the Fourth.

"Blastoff," Harry approves. "Cosmic idea."

"I can borrow it?"

"Well . . . I guess. Yeah. Affirmative. But you'd better be careful of it."

"You wouldn't have a tape of John Philip Sousa marches, would you?"

"Negative. But you can get that downtown. What's your second priority?"

"Your dog."

"What?" Now Harry turns to me.

"There's this scraggly, mangly mutt, Jinny calls him, hangs out at O'Neals'."

"Scraggly mangly . . ."

"I call him Danger Dog. He's dangerous to Sugar. Stalks him when the ponies are loose in Back Field. I thought you might like him."

"You thought I'd like him? Who, me?" Harry sticks his face in mine and pants like an eager dog. "What type of dog is he?"

"Like I said, he's a scraggly mangly . . ."

"Mangly how?"

"Oh. Lost an ear. Limps. Got half a tail."

"What color?"

"Rusty black."

"Batman," says Harry. "Sounds like my dog, all right. I'll call him Dan."

"That's what I thought. Now, take your bad breath away!" Actually, Harry's breath is sweet as Sugar's.

Harry leans back away and wipes his mouth on his sleeve. "When do I come pick up my dog?"

"You'd better come pick up Jan O'Neal first."

"Jan the— Excuse me. Jan the Dreamer. I suppose he's made a treaty with my Dan already."

"Not yet. But he aims to." When Jan lays

eyes on Danger Dog he shifts gear. His head comes up, chin forward. Eyes brighten. Step quickens. He looks like he knows where he's going.

"He's been trying for a close encounter, but so far, no go."

"Hah! With two of us . . . three of us. I'll bring Tom."

Tom Granger was Harry's great pal last summer. He's not Jinny's and my pal.

"Three of us should be able to catch Dan."

I point out, "The hard thing will be taming him."

"You're right." Harry sobers up. "My folks won't let him in the house if he's wild."

"Jan will know how to tame him."

"I hope so, Al. I really hope so. How's your horse programming going?" Harry only asks this to be polite. His thoughtful brown eyes look inward to a vision of Danger Dog, or Dan, all brushed, deflea'ed, and tamed.

"Oh, it's going fine. Cosmic." I don't want to tell trade secrets, even to Harry.

"You get that bridle, Al."

"Bridle?"

"Halter. Whatever. For that wild thing, there."

Lucky looks up from heavy grazing and sees Sugar, half a mile away across purple clover. She neighs to him. Come back here, Baby!

Sugar kicks up his heels and neighs shrilly, you come here, Mom!

She goes, at a canter.

7

May 22
10 A.M.

*H*arry says, "Hey, Al. Hey, Jinny. We want to see Jan."

Tom mutters, "Hey," and looks down at his torn sneakers.

Harry and I have made friends. Harry and Jinny have made peace. But Harry's fat, frowsy friend Tom hasn't been around since we were enemies.

Jinny and I are just coming out of O'Neals' barn, bridles and carrots in hand, to catch our ponies for the day's training. Harry's tape recorder dangles at my waist. I hope he doesn't thing I'm treating it carelessly. This is the only way to carry it, training ponies.

Jinny frowns suspiciously. "Jan? What do you want to see Jan for, Harry Barns?"

"There's this stray dog around here."

"You mean the scraggly mangly mutt."

"We want Jan to help us catch and tame him."

Harry and I don't look at each other. We don't want Tom or Jinny knowing what good friends we are. Tom looks away, down the driveway. "Hey," he says, "hey, look." He points a grubby finger.

Harry grins. "Batman!"

Jinny gives a slight, tight gasp.

Tom stands frozen, pointing. His mouth pouts open.

Up the driveway ambles the most beautiful horse I have ever seen. He's pure white from his delicate, pink nostrils to the tip of his ripply, combed tail. He moves gracefully, bobbing his slender neck like a dancer. He looks at us quietly from wide, dark eyes.

On his back sways the most beautiful girl I have ever seen. Shining golden curls cascade from under her hard hat down her shoulders. Her hacking jacket and jodhpurs and sun-glinting saddle shine, cream-colored. Her tan boots shine. Her slender nose points to the sky.

Jinny murmurs, "Who's this, Princess Di?"

Harry calls, "Hey, Rowan Rich!"

This is the girl Harry told me about. He said she's teaching her horse—this movie-star horse—a trick for the circus. Harry told me she calls him Shah. I know Shah means King.

Tom's pointing finger sinks earthward. Under his wild black curls his brown eyes, watching the princess, soften like butter in sunshine.

Rowan never glances at Tom. She answers Harry's greeting with a short nod and stops Shah with a finger's pressure on his rein.

Shah nods and blows, sedately. It's all I can do to keep my hands still and not pat his white satin shoulder or his slender, soft nose. He smells very sweetly of new-mown hay, grain, and polished leather.

Honolulu. I'm staring at Shah the way dumb Tom is staring at Rowan! I make myself look up at her.

From high above, she tilts her nose down to

study us. In a small, cool voice she asks me, "Are you Jinny O'Neal?"

Jinny barks, "That's me," and sticks her chin out.

The royal gray eyes turn to Jinny. Jinny's jeans have a knee hole, and her coarse, red hair has come loose in back. With an obvious effort, the princess speaks to her politely.

"I'm here to see Mr. O'Neal. Where will I find him?"

"What do you want him for?"

The princess leans a little back away. Her shiny western saddle squeaks. She speaks to Jinny now as she might speak to a small, rude Taylor. "If you must know, I've come here about hay for my horse."

"Oh. Well." That's a horse of a different color. This princess is a Customer. "He's under the pickup," Jinny tells her. "Around to the back."

Rowan stares down at her.

"He's oiling the truck," Jinny explains. "Around back." She points. "My brothers are with him. You'll see a crowd."

Rowan Rich nods and clucks to Shah so

softly I hardly hear her. Instantly, Shah comes to attention and sets off up the driveway.

Stunned, we all turn to watch them round the corner of the barn.

That's how we see Jet and Lucky hanging their common, crude heads over the fence. They must be as astonished by Shah as we are. Not a nicker, not a neigh, escapes them.

A strange silence grips us all till Harry cries, "There he is!"

I ask, "Who?"

"My dog! Look, there he is in the field!"

Harry's right. Well out in the field, Sugar Baby stands trembling as Danger Dog limps toward him. Jet and Lucky, still looking after Shah, do not notice.

I roar, "Get out of there!" and leap to run toward the gate.

Harry grabs and grips my hand. Lucky's carrot bounces on the driveway. "Don't scare him, Al. I want him."

"What'cha mean, 'Don't scare him.' He's after my Sugar!"

Startled, Jet wheels around and sees Danger Dog.

Sugar leaps and gallops toward Lucky and us.

Jet charges after Danger Dog.

Jan wanders out of the barn.

Harry calls out, "Jan O'Neal! Listen—"

Harry lets go of my hand and bounds over to Jan.

Jan pays no attention to Harry. His eyes are on Danger Dog. He straightens up and watches with something like attention as Jet drives Danger Dog across Back Field and under the fence.

Harry talks to Jan a mile a minute.

Jan walks away around the barn, strongly, as if he knows where he's going and why he's going there. Still talking, Harry treads on his heels.

Tom stands rooted till Jinny jeers, "They're going after that dog, Tom. Rowan Rich went thataway, too."

Tom goes after the others.

Jinny chuckles. "That Tom Granger is smitten good! He's got a first-prize coconut on that princess!"

I'm smitten, myself. I've got a coconut on that royal Shah.

I thought we had the circus in our bag. With beautiful Jet and Lucky dancing ballet, and cute little Sugar sashaying along behind, how could we lose? I could taste those five hundred dollars! I just knew we were going to win, the way I knew this was Saturday morning.

That was before I saw the king and princess.

"Come on." Jinny swings her bridle. "We've got a circus to train for."

She starts off toward our ponies.

I pick up Lucky's carrot and follow, slower.

I'm thinking. Sugar needs a halter. I've priced it at the feed store. It won't be cheap.

I've borrowed Harry's tape recorder.

And yet, after all this, there's still a chance we maybe might not win.

* * * * * * * * * * * * 8

June 5
10 A.M.

Al," Dad says, "you're not such a chickweed after all!" And he sort of smiles. I sort of smile back.

We are weeding Dad's goldenrods and tiger lilies around our front gate. They're still just green stalks about a foot high. But Dad loves his strong, tall flowers. He raises flowers other people call weeds: ironweeds, mullein, joe-pye weed. He weeds them as carefully as Grandma weeds her carrots and beets out back. Today I offered to help.

Here we kneel together inside the open gate, pulling weeds. Robins and catbirds sing, and swallows swoop around the sky. We shake useful dirt off the roots and pile the weeds in the wheelbarrow. Dad has on his oldest patched jeans and denim shirt, and a half-smile on his face. He smiles most often among his flowers.

I ask, "Why would I be a chickweed, anyhow?"

"Well, you know, you're completely pony mad." Dad talks to the goldenrods, head down, so I can't see his eyes. "You're pretty good with your grandma, but I don't often get a lick of work out of you."

True. "Well, you're not around much, Dad."

"I know you can work, though. You're a good baby-sitter, and that takes stick-with-it. Anyone who can stick with those Taylor kids . . . I've heard about them."

There are four Taylor kids under seven and they're all Dennis the Menaces.

"And you've kept your pony, What's-its-name—"

"Lucky."

"You kept it fed all winter. That took some doing."

Dad tosses two handfuls of weeds in the wheelbarrow and claps his hard hands clean.

Listening to this list of my good points, I have forgotten to weed. I kneel here with my jaw practically hanging. Dad looks up at me and I see his gray eyes, kind as Jet's eyes. Kind as Harry's. Dad and I are talking, and he's saying good things about me, and he looks at me as though he really likes me! I can't believe this wonderful, rainbow-type moment!

"Fact is, Al, I've realized something. I've got an all-round pretty good daughter. A regular ironweed!" What praise could be higher, from Dad? "And I don't notice her enough."

I gurgle my astonishment.

"I'm sorry I get so busy sometimes I can't hardly see you."

This is just all too much! I mutter, "Oh, Dad! I know you're busy."

"Darned right I'm busy! One day you'll know what it takes to keep a show like this going." He looks out past me at the house, Grandma coming around the house, the yard . . .

I knew it was all too good to last.

Dad's eyes widen. His half-smile fades. A scowl darkens his face. His hands clench.

"What," he growls, "is that?"

Fearfully, I look over my shoulder.

Jinx trots gently, swiftly, past my heels toward the gate. A tiny black something dangles, wiggling from her jaws.

I whisper, "Could be a mole."

Furious, Dad whispers, "Could be, but ain't!"

Jinx pauses, one forefoot high, and looks at Dad.

Dad leaps to his feet.

Jinx darts through the gate and vanishes in the long grass by the road.

Blastoff!

All in a second, the sun stops shining. The world goes dark. Dad glowers down at me. His clenched fists tremble. "You knew about this, Al!"

"Well . . . uh . . ."

"It's been going on behind my back. That kitten's a good month old."

"Three weeks. We couldn't help it, Dad. They just happened."

Like Sugar just happened.

Dad looks over at Grandma, who is coming toward us from her garden. He shouts, "Mom!"

Grandma hears that perfectly. She stops in her tracks.

"Oh, heavens," she quavers. "Did you see . . ."

Dad strides over to Grandma. I pick myself up and follow. Loudly, face thrust close to hers, Dad scolds Grandma. She can only say what I said. "What could we do, Dave? God made them."

"How many? How many cats?"

"Seven." Actually, there would be six now, if we hadn't fed the black runt extra. We call him Hex, and he's our favorite.

"Seven cats to feed! Eight, with the mother!" From behind Dad, I watch rage jerk his sharp shoulders.

Grandma holds her white head high. "I've got my embroidery money, Dave."

"Eight cats to stumble over on a dark winter morning."

"I'll find them homes. I've got some ideas right now."

Slowly, Dad's hands unclench. Slower, his shoulders loosen. "Well. What's done is done."

Dad's anger is like a tornado. It rips through our life and disappears. But, Honolulu! If a kitten the size of a field mouse can upset Dad this much, he'd better not meet Sugar till the parade. And Sugar had better win us that five hundred dollars!

* * * * * * * * * * * * * **9**

I turn on Harry's tape recorder at my waist, and John Philip Sousa blares forth with trumpets, cymbals, and drums. Our Song.

Lucky bridles and sidles, pricks ears, swishes tail. From the beginning of training, John Philip Sousa has had a strong effect on her.

I reign her in and call out to Jinny, six yards away on Jet. "Remember when you could just whistle and scare Lucky into the next field?"

"I sure do! We've come a long way."

Sugar Baby whinnies and bucks. A long lead

ties his new halter to a rope around Lucky's middle. A loose-woven chain of purple-and-white clover flops around his neck. Someone keeps dressing Sugar up in wildflowers when I'm not looking. It's sort of cute.

Sugar is tamer than he used to be, but that doesn't mean he's tame. Not yet. We tie him up beside Lucky when I brush her. Then I brush him and lead him around Back Field. If he balks, Jinny wraps an old bath towel around his rear and pulls him along. He's a lot stronger then he looks.

"Never lose your temper with a horse," Dad told me. With Sugar, it's right hard not to! He's stubborn as a donkey and sulky as a Taylor after a tantrum. Sometimes I forget how cute he is and swear at him sweetly. He doesn't know I'm swearing.

When we program Jet and Lucky, Sugar gets led along, too. After all, he will be in the act with them. "He's learning," Jinny tells me confidently every day. "He's coming along."

Now Jinny calls, "Start it over, Al. We missed the opening."

I switch the tape off. A surprisingly nice silence opens around us. Faintly, from far trees,

I hear robins sing. Lucky blows and reaches down for grass.

I bring her up short. "Attention, Lucky! All set, Jinny?"

"All set over here."

I switch the tape on.

Lucky's ears perk forward. I feel her tense.

I press my heels against her sides. She steps forward smartly.

"That's right, girl! One, two, three, pause." I drag on the reins. Lucky pauses in place. I glance over and see Jet paused, one forefoot raised, chin pulled right into his chest. I release the reins and press Lucky forward again. "One, two, three, pau-au-au-ause." Again, Jet has kept pace.

Around Back Field we dance, one, two, three, pause. From the middle of the field, Cow watches us. John Philip does something to her, too. Her hairy ears wave at us, and she keeps turning to face us.

The tape is long. When it ends we are half-way round the field. The barn and house look small from here.

I switch off the tape and just sit, breathing

in the silence. Jinny nudges Jet over beside us, and the three ponies nuzzle each other.

"It's getting good," Jinny says. "But you know, they have to do it themselves."

"You mean, without us reining in and kicking."

"Affirmative."

I think over what Dad said. "Okay, we can't rein in and kick, but maybe we can do something else."

"Like how?"

"Like . . . like this." I lean forward and tap Lucky's neck with a finger. "I'll tap like this every time I rein in. Pretty soon, if I just tap, Lucky will think I'm reining in. You do it, too."

Jinny shrugs. "Can't hurt to try. Start it up, Al."

On comes John Philip Sousa. Lucky tenses, perks her ears—and steps out without being told! One, two, three, tap. Rein. Pause. One, two, three, tap, rein, pause. I call to Jinny over the trombones, "She's doing it!"

Actually, Lucky has learned that Our Song means Step Forward Smartly, one, two, three. Jet learns more slowly. Maybe that's because he's older.

Gradually the barn and house grow bigger as

we follow the fence around to the gate. Cow turns with us, head high, ears waving, until at last the tape ends. Then she goes back to her grazing.

"Enough, already!" Jinny complains.

"Affirmative." I'm not sure who is getting programmed here. The world sure sounds good without John Philip! I'm dizzy from doing one, two, three, pause.

Now I can hear other sounds. Like shod hoofs on gravel.

Jinny says softly, "Hey!"

Across the gate, I see a white blur.

Very softly, Jinny says, "It's the princess."

My head stops whirling. I see Rowan. She's sitting Shah outside the closed barn door, looking calmly around her. Beautiful Shah stands like a marble horse on a pedestal, shining white in the sun.

Jinny shouts, "Hey, Rowan, you want more hay?"

The princess and Shah just look at us.

Jinny jumps down off Jet and climbs over the gate.

I slide down from Lucky and tie her reins to

the fence. Then I walk through the gate, shutting it behind me like a responsible person.

Jinny is already at Rowan's stirrup.

Rowan is saying, "Actually, I'm looking for your brother."

"Which brother? I've got three. There's Jack—"

"I'm looking for the . . . the animal trainer."

"That's Jan," Jinny informs her. "He's in there." She points at the closed barn door. "You want him to train your hay-chomper?"

Rowan looks down at Jinny the way Sugar looks at me when he's good and tired of me. "Actually, it's Jan's friend I want to see. Are his friends in there with him now?"

"I wouldn't know," Jinny says. "They generally are, this time of day."

Rowan Rich wants to see Harry?

Why?

Suddenly, I realize I dislike Rowan's cool manner and royal beauty. I dislike her shiny hard hat, cream coat, and soft new boots. I dislike her attitude.

I say, "I'll find out. You stay here." I brush past Shah's soft, velvet nose and open the barn door and walk in.

Danger Dog—I mean, Dan—barks like a suspicious watchdog.

"No fair!" Tom Granger shouts. "You can't see our trick!"

Tom, Harry, and Jan sit cross-legged in sawdust with Dan and Ring in the middle. Jan bounces a tennis ball slowly from one hand to the other. Ring sits up and reaches his little paws as if to catch it. Jan does not seem to see me.

Tom and Harry jump up and turn to me. Tom's face lights up like a candle. He sees Rowan and Shah behind me, in the sunlight.

Harry sees them, too. I'm glad to see that his face does not change.

I say, "Rowan wants to see you."

"Us? Why?" Harry looks only puzzled.

Tom stumbles past me to Rowan like a zombie.

"Why does she want us?" Harry asks me again.

"Come on out and ask her."

Harry tells Jan, "Just a sec." Jan pays no attention, never looks up. Together, Harry and I walk out into the sunshine.

Rowan is saying to Tom, "I just want you. Come with me. I'll show you."

"Sure," Tom mutters, like he's hypnotized on TV.

"This way." Rowan gathers her reins and leans sideways. Shah comes to life, wheels around, and ambles off down the driveway. Rowan never looks back to see if Tom follows.

Tom gives Harry an embarrassed look. "Gotta go," he says.

Harry nods. "Go ahead."

Tom says, "See . . . it's like . . ."

"Go on."

Tom goes.

Harry, Jinny, and I watch them turn right, down O'Neals' Hill. Harry sighs. "Guess you've noticed, Tom's got a real, whole coconut."

Jinny guffaws. "Is that what you call it?"

I've got a coconut, too. For Shah. How sweetly he takes orders! How gently he steps! His shod hoofs hardly grind the driveway gravel. I wonder what trick Rowan is teaching him.

When we win the circus and the five hundred dollars, I'll buy a hard hat like Rowan's. And soft, new boots.

* * * * * * * * * * * * **10**

*H*onolulu!" Jinny whirls around our rain-dark kitchen like a red-white-and-blue tornado. Her blue satin slipper-toes hardly seem to touch the floor. "Mrs. Brown, these costumes are just great! They're blastoff!"

I look down at myself a bit doubtfully. I'm not used to showing quite this much of me in public.

The costumes hang low on the chest from very thin, almost invisible, shoulder straps. Each has a red strip first, then a white strip, then an elastic waist, then a red strip, then a puffy blue hem ending halfway up the thigh, with little blue panties underneath. It will be like wearing a bathing suit on Main Street. There's red-white-and-blue striped bows at the waist in back and in our hair. Our slippers are blue.

I say loudly, "They're not going to be much fun riding in, Grandma." Too much bare skin to rub against horse hair!

Grandma says, "You can stand it for an hour." She smiles proudly at us across her sewing machine and hums, "I Got Shoes."

Little black Hex jumps from her lap to the table and commences batting scraps around. The other kitties chase and pounce under the table. They're all indoors with us because of the rain.

At the other end of the table Dad studies the gardening page of the *Granton Enquirer*, coffee at hand. His Saturday gardening is being rained out, but he can still dream. Hex better not bat the paper or spill the coffee!

"Dave," Grandma calls to him down the table. "What do you think of the girls' costumes?"

Dad looks up vaguely. It takes him a minute to really see and notice us.

"Spiffy!" he declares. "Regular circus stuff. If they don't fall off during the act."

"Fall off?" Anxiety dims Grandma's bright face. She turns to us. "Girls, hop around a bit. See if the costumes feel like falling off."

Jinny whirls from fridge to TV to stove.

I take a step, and another, and twirl around. I'm heavier than Jinny. I do it again and feel lighter. Again, and I gallop about the kitchen like Sugar playing in sunlight.

"How do they feel?" Grandma calls.

I gasp, "Fine!"

There's no danger my costume will fall. My skirt puffs out like a tutu. My big bows flutter like butterflies. I dance to the drumming of rain on the windows.

Dad says approvingly, "Your costumes are winners, Mom."

Spinning and fluttering, I feel we will be winners. Since school let out we've been spending every spare minute programming ponies, and they're getting a passing grade. Even Sugar gets a C for effort! We've taken them downtown three times, to get them used to people and cars. They will act right in the parade. With Sugar's help we really will win the five hundred dollars.

The princess and Shah will be serious competition. But Shah won't win just by being beautiful. This will be a circus, not a horse show.

Harry and Tom and Jan have been training Dan and Ring Coon in the barn. Jan knows what he's doing. They will be serious competition.

But we will be better. We will win.

I'm dizzy. Fridge and stove swim past me. I grab hold of the pantry door before the floor hits me.

When I win, I will sell my common, crude ponies and buy an Arabian horse. He will be beautiful, graceful, and perfectly trained. He will stop at the pressure of my finger on a rein. He will start at my whisper.

The kitchen slows down and stops spinning.

I bite my lip, not to speak. This is not something I can say aloud to anyone, this dark, secret thought. Jinny would laugh at the thought of me selling my miracle ponies. Grandma would be shocked. Dad doesn't think my

Lucky is worth money. He'll be surprised that I can sell her.

Well, Dad is going to be surprised, anyway. When he sees Sugar in the parade . . . Hastily, my thoughts fast-forward to when he sees us win the five hundred dollars.

Yes, Dad will be surprised.

Now he asks me, "Will your ponies be dolled up to match you?"

"Certainly!" Grandma gloats. "I've got ribbons and bells for them, too."

I say, "And flower wreaths. Somebody will do that, they always do."

"What?" Both Dad and Grandma stare.

Jinny scowls at me.

I swallow hard. How do I explain without telling about Sugar? Like this. "Well, there's somebody comes when we're not looking and drapes wildflower wreathes on . . . the ponies."

Dad comments, "Hah!"

Grandma says brightly, "A pixie!"

"What, Grandma?" I show her a puzzled face.

"Like the shoemaker and the elves, you know. You remember, the elves made the shoes at night while the shoemaker slept."

75

"Oh." I think I get it.

"Elves, pixies, what-you-call-'ems, you've got one."

"Sure, Grandma."

"One thing," Dad puts in. "What happens if it rains on July Fourth?"

"What say?" Grandma frowns and leans forward over the sewing machine.

"What if it rains like this on the big day?" Holy horror, what a thought!

"Oh, no!" Grandma leans back confidently. "The sun always shines on the Fourth."

Hex pounces on Dad's paper and knocks over his coffee.

Dad grunts angrily. "Mom," he says loudly, "these cats have got to go."

"You know what, Dave, I've got that planned. I'll sell them at the parade."

"You'll what?"

"I'll find them all homes at the parade. I'll take them down in a basket and hand them out left and right. 'Train these kittens for next year's circus,' I'll say. 'Win a big prize!' "

Dad's rare laughter rings out over the rattling rain.

11

July 4
7:30 A.M.

*H*onolulu, the sun's shining!" Jinny almost sings as I lead my ponies into the barn, one pony on each hand. Lucky walks smoothly now, not pulling back or snapping at me. Sugar comes where he is led, sulkily.

(My new Arabian horse I'm going to buy will never sulk. I won't miss this stubborn colt. Just let him win us the five hundred dollars, and it'll be good-bye, baby.)

Old Jet stands cross-tied between uprights. He shines like black plastic. His black tail is tightly braided. Jinny is braiding his mane into parallel plaits down his neck on one side.

"How long have you been grooming Jet?"

"Hours. Now it's time for the finishing touches."

"Here they are. And our costumes." I set down the shopping bag of ribbons, bells, and costumes that Grandma gave me.

Jinny paws through it eagerly. "Can I have the silver bows? Silver looks great with black."

"Sure. I'll take the blue ones."

Jet nods and knocks a front hoof on the floor. "Easy, boy. . . . Just two more braids here. . . . Al, you'd better get busy. You remembered the tape recorder, I hope."

"Affirmative."

"Without that we'd be lost!"

Quickly I cross-tie Lucky nose to nose with Jet with Sugar Baby at her tail. I commence brushing.

"Oof!" Jinny cries, disgusted. "Move away! Lucky's getting dust on Jet."

She's right. Tiny specks float in the air and dim Jet's glorious face already.

"Sorry."

Lucky and I back up ten feet, retie, and start over.

Jinny says, "You're going to doll Sugar up, I hope. He has to charm the judges. You know what he needs? Daisy chains. Like the pixie puts on him when we're not looking."

Too bad the pixie didn't deck Sugar out this time! "Right. I'll pick daisies on the way." They grow thick among purple clovers along O'Neal Road.

"One chain around his neck," Jinny murmurs, braiding. "And one down his tail, and . . . He'll be tied to Lucky, won't he?"

"That's one sure thing." I'm not going to chase Sugar through a screaming crowd.

Jinny pauses a moment. "Hey! What if your dad sees Sugar, as we go by the house?"

I shrug. "No problem. He and Sugar are due to meet today anyhow." Only it might be a happier occasion if it happened after Sugar won the five hundred dollars.

Lucky shakes mane and tail and stamps impatiently. One golden brown eye glows at me.

Jinny says, "They know something's up."

"Sure. They feel we're excited."

"These sure are two smart ponies . . . I mean, three smart ponies."

Excitement bursts out of me. "You know what I'll do when I win, Jinny?"

"You said. If we win, you'll buy a saddle."

"More than that. I'm going to sell these two and buy me an Arabian!"

Lucky rubs her forehead up and down my shoulder. Sugar half-rears against his rope and whinnies.

"What?" Jinny pauses, tying silver bows to Jet's plaits. "I didn't get that."

"I'm going to sell these two—"

"And buy an Arabian! Hah!" Jinny laughs shortly and bends to her work.

"I am. I will."

"You know how much an Arabian costs?"

"How much?"

"Too much and then some. And he wouldn't be a miracle horse, either."

That's true. I brush Lucky's glossy shoulder. Lucky is my miracle rainbow pony. And today she's going to win five hundred dollars.

"You're a real clown, Al," Jinny declares. "I bet you thought I believed you."

Okay. I let it go at that. Jinny really wouldn't

understand my wanting to sell Lucky or even thinking of it! She herself would never dream of selling old Jet.

"Snap along," she says. "We've still got to doll ourselves up. I'll help you braid."

"Lucky's going loose." Lucky's milkweed fluff mane and tail, which sail on the wind, are her best features.

"You aren't going to braid?" Jinny flies into orbit. "Al, we've got to look the same!"

"No need."

"Al Brown, either you braid or—"

"Jinny O'Neal, don't you go into overdrive!"

"Hey," says a deep voice from the doorway. We turn as one.

Harry says, "We're here for Jan and Ring." Dan, alert at Harry's heels, wears a new red collar.

Jinny echoes, "We?"

"My uncle's driving us. Hi, Jan."

Jan shuffles out of the big, dim barn behind us. His jeans and shirt look ironed. His thick dark hair is combed. Ring Coon peers at us around his red-scrubbed neck. In clean hands, Jan carries a fresh, shining daisy chain.

"Come on," Harry urges him. "Time to go!"

Jan shambles up to Sugar Baby. Sugar whuffles at him and pushes his forehead against Jan's clean shirt. They're good friends, Jan and my Sugar Baby.

Jan raises the daisy chain high and lowers it gently around Sugar's slender neck.

Jan is our pixie. Of course. Naturally. Why didn't we guess?

"Okay," Harry tells Jan, almost impatiently. "That's enough fraternizing with the enemy. Let's go!" He nods at Jet and Lucky. "Horses look snappy. Hey, Al, take care of my tape recorder."

"Don't frazzle yourself, Harry. It's safe with me."

Harry turns to go.

"Harry!" I surprise myself, calling him back.

Harry turns back.

"What do you think? If Jet has braids, should Lucky have them, too?"

Jinny mutters, "He's the enemy, dumbie!" This is the second mention of enemies in two minutes. I'm not sure I like this.

Harry looks from one pony to the other and back. "Affirmative," he decides. "Looks more like a team, makes more impression, if they look the same."

"Thanks, Harry."

Surprised, Jinny mutters, "Good luck."

Harry grins and goes, Jan and Dan on his heels.

I sigh. "Well, Jinny O'Neal, which shall it be? Braids or loose?"

"Honolulu! I'm not brushing out all those braids!"

"Okay. Help me braid."

This is no time for us to fight.

* * * * * * * * * * * * **12**

July 4
10:30 A.M.

Up ahead the bass drum booms. The high school band strikes up with fife, cymbal, and trumpet. The flag lurches forward. At the tail end of the parade, we sit our nervous ponies.

Lucky nods, paws, and circles in place, jingling her bells. I hold her in hard. Jet arches and blows, shifting from side to side. Behind us, Rowan sits Shah coolly, nose in air. She wears no costume, just her usual crisp cream outfit and hard hat.

A fat clown with a little red wagon stands at Rowan's shiny stirrup. He sweats and shifts his ballooning weight from one foot to the other. Looking twice through his painted grin, I see that he is Tom. So! Tom completely deserted Harry and Jan and took up with the princess!

Behind them stand Harry and Jan, with Ring Coon on Jan's shoulder. Dan sits beside Harry, panting loudly. I'm happy to see he's been well bathed, deflea'ed, brushed, and fed. He looks happy but not handsome. Jinny can still call him a scruffy, mangled mutt.

Behind them, other animal acts wait in line. Dogs, two goat kids, a caged parrot, a covered basket. A covered basket? I catch Jinny's eye and nod at the basket. Jinny shrugs and grins.

The high school band marches first. Then go the flag and the Veterans, then the police cars and fire trucks, while we wait. I wonder what would happen to Granton, Massachusetts, if a fire or big crime broke out right now? It would take a while to get out through this crowd!

Next go the little kids with decorated bicycles and/or storybook costumes. Jinny and I used to march with them. They pause at the reviewing stand to be judged, while we wait.

Impatient Lucky circles and tosses her braids, bells jingling. Tied to her tail, Sugar Baby trembles. He had a long walk down O'Neal's Hill and through town, and the crowd scares him. Sweat shines on his curly red coat. The daisy chains on his neck, mane, and tail wilt. I'm kind of sorry he has to be here. But of course, we need him to charm the judges. Hey, I hope the judges aren't sorry for him!

At last the little kids are judged. Now the floats creak slowly forward while we wait. These are stagelike scenes set up on truckbeds, drawn by choking, growling engines. The exhausts blow right in our faces. We have to turn the ponies clean around backward to breathe. Up ahead, the crowd laughs and whistles at the floats. They stop and get judged while we wait.

Now at last it's our turn.

I mutter in Lucky's alert ear, "Here we go," and loosen rein a bit.

Side by side, Jet and Lucky march forward. I glance down at Sugar, wobbling alongside. "Ooooh," says the crowd, on either side. "Loook! Isn't he cuuute!" Just as I had hoped.

Here and there I see faces I know. Kids from school, parents we baby-sit for. Two Taylor kids are hugging little tricolored kittens. Grandma's been handing them out.

Jinny's brothers Jack and Jerry wave to us.

There's Grandma with two friends, all in red-blue-and-white outfits. She grins and waves to us.

There's Dad.

He stands alone in a little clearing in the crowd, arms folded, head high. He nods to me gravely. Pacing past, I nod back.

His eyes widen, then narrow sharply. He rises on tiptoe. He has seen Sugar, dragged along at Lucky's tail.

My heart pounds like the kettledrum.

I set my eyes sternly ahead and march on.

At the reviewing stand we pause.

The band stops playing.

Up on the platform stand three judges and the MC, the Master of Ceremonies. The MC waves signals to us. Following his directions, we march round in a big circle and stop, facing the stand.

I count eight acts in all. Six kids and two

teenagers, all wanting that five hundred dollars, which, of course, I'm going to win.

The MC reads a speech into the microphone, all about the first priority Granton Alive effort and the five hundred dollars. The crowd moves in around and among us.

The MC booms, "First: Jinny O'Neal and Alice Brown with Jet, Lucky, and Sugar." He nods to us. This is it.

* * * * * * * * * * * * **13**

*J*inny and I exchange one determined glance.

I switch on the tape recorder at my waist. John Philip Sousa blares forth with trumpets and cymbals. This is Our Song.

Lucky knows Our Song. She paws, nods, shifts her weight. Her bells clang. Her ears point straight up into the music. Will she dance?

I nudge her with slippered heels.

Lucky steps forward. Jet steps forward. The dance commences.

Together we pace around the circle, three steps, pause, three steps, pause. I tap Lucky's shoulder to remind her to pause. After a few pauses Lucky hits cruising gear. She steps high, and her braids bounce. She doesn't really need my taps anymore, but I still give them. Can't take a chance. "Ahhh!" breathes the crowd.

I thought I might be nervous in front of people. But now we're here, I hardly see them. All I see is Lucky's perky ears and bouncing braids. I'm too busy counting steps to think about the crowd.

Back at the starting point Jet moves ahead. Jet is not quite in Lucky's gear. His tight-braided tail droops, and he steps almost sulkily.

I glance down at Sugar and almost lose the beat. He wobbles at Lucky's heels, head low. Do I hear sympathetic moans from the crowd? Sugar Baby, don't you dare lose us this prize!

Halfway round the circle Jet wheels back the other way, three steps, pause. Lucky goes ahead, three steps, pause. During programming we have sometimes lost synch at this moment. Not this time.

Lucky and I are almost back to the starting point. Here comes Jet, waltzing to meet us. I wheel Lucky around, and we part company. Back at the halfway point, Jet meets us again.

We circle each other, right, then left. Sugar Baby staggers a tight circle in the middle. We programmed to repeat the whole performance from here, but I don't think Sugar would make it. I signal Jinny to fast-forward. We draw rein side by side, facing the MC and the judges, and I turn off the tape.

Together we scramble up to stand on the ponies' backs.

That rumbling noise is the crowd, clapping.

Together we bow, left and right, and grin to sell toothpaste.

Together we jump down.

Programming, we've always jumped down onto earth. This paved road slaps our slippered feet with a right smart jolt. That's one thing we hadn't prepared for.

Another thing we hadn't prepared for, my waistband breaks. The tape recorder crashes to the pavement and self-destructs. Blastoff, its innards are all around my feet and rolling into the crowd.

Should I gather it up and spoil our grand exit?

Jinny hisses, "Smile! Smile, you Reject!"

Grinning like clowns, we limp out of the circle, leading the ponies.

The crowd roars appreciation. If my feet and the insides of my legs didn't sting so awfully, that roar would lift me to heaven.

We must have won! Of course we've won, in spite of pitiful Sugar Baby!

We face the ponies toward the circle and climb back aboard. Can't very well stand anymore on these smarting feet!

The MC has been barking something I didn't hear. Now it's the princess's turn.

Proud, stone-faced, she rides magnificent Shah into the center. Their combined beauty is absolutely cosmic. Stunning. The crowd gasps.

Fine. But you'll need more than looks, Princess. This here's a circus, not a horse show.

Shah goes into a little side-step dance more complex than ours. He arches his graceful neck, swings two steps right, and skips. He arches, steps left, and skips. Rowan sits in her western saddle like she's bored, nose in air, giving no directions at all. I can't even see her knees or heels tighten to remind Shah of the step. Our dumb ponies needed more encouragement than that.

Now Tom Clown leaps out of the crowd. The little red wagon clatters after him, tied to his sagging sash. Waving a kid's shovel, he scoops up invisible manure. Some of this invisible manure lands in the wagon, and some under Shah's nodding nose. The crowd snickers.

Shah never misses a step.

Tom dances and cavorts and shovels, clatters his wagon and bangs his shovel. He pulls a little drum out of his clown pants and rumbles it in front of Shah.

Shah never misses a step.

"Blastoff," Jinny murmurs. "I never thought that Tom Granger could work so hard!"

Shah dances, arch, step, skip. His midnight eyes never seem to blink. Rowan rides stonefaced, blind to Tom's antics. The crowd laughs now, loud and louder.

Three times Shah circles the ring while Tom tries to fluster him. Then Rowan rides him calmly out and away. Tom whirls around shoveling invisible manure before he, too, disappears in the laughing, clapping crowd.

I'm stunned. This coarse, comic act is far from what I expected of the princess. That Rowan Rich is smarter at show business than I thought!

Jinny mutters, "That's okay. We've got Sugar Baby."

She right. No clown shoveling manure could compete with my Sugar Baby if he was on his twinkling toes. I look down and catch him drooping, his coat all shiny with sweat. You've let me down, Sugar! You've let me down bad.

The MC barks, "Next, we have Jan O'Neal, Ring, Harry Barns, and Dan."

Harry steps out boldly, Dan at his heels. Jan wanders, smiling, into the circle, Ring balanced on his shoulder. The crowd murmurs curiously.

"No costumes," Jinny mutters. "That'll cut them down with the judges, right there."

Harry gives a hand signal. Dan and Ring sit in front of him and look up, bright-eyed.

No one could call Dan a handsome dog. But such intelligence shines in his brown eyes, gazing up at Harry, that I groan out loud.

"Shhh!" Jinny scolds. She reaches out a slippered foot and kicks my shin.

Harry lifts a small beanbag from his jeans pocket and holds it high. Ring sits up on his stump-tail and waves his clever hands. Dan jumps up.

"No," says Harry. "Down." He still holds the beanbag high. Dan sits back down, panting. Harry waits a second, then gives a hand signal. Dan barks.

"Okay," says Harry. He tosses the beanbag out into the ring.

Now Harry folds his arms and watches like one of the crowd as Dan and Ring scramble after that beanbag.

You'd think they would pounce on it and tear it and each other in bits.

But what they do is, they kick it around the circle the way two kids will kick a pebble, each one trying to keep it for himself. The crowd murmurs and laughs.

Jinny mutters, "Holy horrors!" I reach and kick her shin.

Jan claps his hands.

Instantly, Dan and Ring quit with the beanbag. They run to Jan and sit at his feet.

Jan brings a tennis ball out of his pocket. He

bounces and catches it twice. Then he tosses it gently to Ring.

Ring catches that ball in his hands.

The crowd shouts.

Ring places the ball on the ground and pushes it to Dan. Dan stops it with his paw and pushes it back to Ring. Away and around they go, rolling that tennis ball back and forth between them.

The crowd roars.

I'm going to be sick.

Jinny says, "It's okay. It's perfectly okay. We've got Sugar."

I look down at Sugar. Pressed close to Lucky's shoulder, he wilts like his daisy chains.

Harry and Jan collect their animals. Harry bows to the whooping crowd. Jan backs away into the crowd, Ring in his arms, till Mr. O'Neal's hand comes down on his shoulder.

The next act is a husky boy with the covered basket. He uncovers the basket and sits down cross-legged beside it. He pulls a pipe out of his shirt and blows it, shrill and flat.

The crowd takes a giant step back.

Slowly, a shiny black, cold-eyed head rises a

foot above the basket. The crowd takes another giant step back.

The kid tootles away on his pipe.

He's got a medium-size black snake in that basket. I've seen them on O'Neal's Hill, sunning on rocks. Once I saw a huge one hurl himself up in the air and dive into a blueberry thicket. My dad says they can go faster than we humans.

Uneasy, I draw Lucky back away.

But the snake rises no farther out of the basket. The kid tootles and sways. He does the dance okay, but the snake just looks on. Finally the snake gets bored and sinks down again for a snooze.

After a few last, desperate tootles the kid picks up his basket and slouches off down a wide path in the crowd.

"Honolulu!" Jinny breathes. "That one could have carried off the cake if it worked."

I agree. Not even Sugar could have outdone that black snake if he had danced. But he didn't. I'm going to win. I'm going to win. I have to win.

Dogs follow, then the goat kids, and finally

the parrot, who carries on a recognizable Who's On First routine.

None of these acts bother me. I'd still win hands down if it weren't for Harry and Jan, and maybe Shah. I admit, they bother me.

"Buck up," Jinny whispers, nudging my leg with hers. "We've got more than a fighting chance. You know, I'm seeing Jinx's kittens everywhere I look."

I glance around. Black-and-white kittens nestle in several kids' arms. Grandma's doing well.

The MC commences to bark.

All of us contestants move into the circle, listening with all our ears. Across the circle I see Jan with Mr. O'Neal, Harry, and Rowan, bored and superior, on Shah.

One awful thought nags at me. This was an Animal Act. The animals were supposed to do it. Well, Shah did it, and Ring and Dan did it. But our dumb ponies didn't really do that much. Jinny and I guided them through our trick. Jinny and I did it.

But we've got Sugar Baby. We'll win, yet. I've got to win.

The MC has been consulting with the judges. Now he turns back to us. In his hands he holds three large ribbon bows and a long, slender envelope. In that envelope there must be a check for five hundred dollars.

Here we go. Now we find out who gets the five hundred dollars, the saddle, jodhpurs and boots, the Arabian horse.

I watch the MC's lips open, like Grandma would. Like her, I watch and hear the fateful words fall.

14

July 4
12:15 P.M.

Shhh!" says everyone. The crowd listens.

My throat hurts. Cymbals clash in my chest.

I've got to win, got to win, got to win. Sell these dumb, dumb ponies and buy—

"Third prize, white ribbon," the MC roars through the microphone. He holds high a huge, white, shiny bow. "Third prize, honorable mention, goes to . . ."

"Shhhhh!"

"Ernie Smith with Costello Abbott!"

That's the parrot in the cage. Ernie Smith carries the cage up on the platform, takes the white bow from the smiling MC, and hangs it on the cage. Then he jumps down into the clapping crowd.

"Whew!" Jinny says. "Not us!" We didn't want third prize, so I guess that's good.

"Second prize," roars the MC. "Red ribbon, honorable mention, goes to Rowan Rich on Shah, with Tom Granger."

"Hah!" Jinny breathes. "Still not us."

Still good.

Stone-faced, Rowan rides Shah up to the platform. Tom cavorts alongside, clattering his little red wagon. The MC hands down Rowan's red ribbon, which she hangs in Shah's mane. At a flick of her finger, Shah moves gently away through the admiring crowd. No one speaks to Rowan, but Tom gets blocked and stopped by congratulating friends.

Now. "First prize. Blue ribbon. Five hundred dollars." The MC shakes the blue bow in one hand and the long, slender envelope in the other, over his head. The envelope swims before my fainting eyes.

"First prize, blue ribbon, five hundred dollars, goes to . . . ah . . ."—the MC turns to mumble with a judge—". . . ah, first prize goes to Jan O'Neal and Harry Barns, with Ring and Dan."

Wild clapping. Shouts. Boots stamp.

No.

Harry gets to climb on the reviewing stand with Dan and shake hands with the MC and the three judges.

No.

Jan watches vaguely from the sidelines.

The MC gestures him up there, too.

Mr. O'Neal presses and pats his shoulder and points to the platform.

Mrs. O'Neal pushes through the crowd to Jan. She points to the platform and speaks sharply, I can tell from her face.

Harry waves and beckons.

Jan stands there watching vaguely.

"Jan O'Neal," the MC booms. "Come up and get your prize, Jan O'Neal."

A judge taps the MC on the shoulder and murmurs in his ear.

"Oh, well," the MC says aloud, half in the microphone, "in that case maybe—"

Harry bends down and speaks to Dan.

Dan bounds off the platform. Sunshine glints off his new, red collar as he streaks to Jan, sits down before him and barks.

Jan wakes up. He looks down at Dan and up at the platform. He sees Harry waving wildly. Slowly, he steps out from under Mr. O'Neal's hand and ambles up to the platform. Ring Coon on his shoulder, Dan at his heels, he climbs the steps and stands beside Harry.

No.

The crowd roars, laughs, even cries. Looking around, I see a tear creep down a cheek here and there. I can't think why.

No tear creeps down my cheek, I'll say that for me. Even though we haven't won. Even though we've lost. Right now, in front of my eyes, Harry is about to take the long, thin white envelope from the MC.

No.

First, Jan gets the blue ribbon. He marvels at it, holds it up in the light and looks at it from different sides. Now he sits down, right there on the platform with everybody watching. He lifts Ring Coon from his shoulder to his lap. He ties the blue ribbon to Ring's ringed tail.

Now cameras flash as the MC hands Harry

the long, thin envelope. "What are you going to do with your share of the prize money?" he shouts in the microphone.

Harry murmurs something.

"What? Say that again." The MC pushes the mike toward Harry.

Harry shouts, "I'm going to buy dog food."

The crowd loves that.

"Now," the MC rumbles, "the Fourth of July Committee invites you one and all to stick around for the barbecue and the baseball game and . . ."

It's over. That's it. We're through.

I blink back tears and gulp down rage.

A lean man stands beside Lucky and looks at Sugar.

"Dad."

He gives me his rare, wonderful smile. How can he smile? We didn't win.

"He's great," says Dad.

"Oh." He means Sugar. "Yes. He is."

"You must have been excited when he was born. I'd say, about three months ago."

"Yes. During that sugar-snow storm."

Dad reaches a friendly hand to Sugar. "Hey, big fellow . . ."

Sugar is so tired now, he stands and lets Dad touch, then rub, his slender forehead. I've never seen Dad so friendly to anything on four legs!

He says, "He's a beauty, Al. I see you got him a halter, trained him some."

"Like you said to do."

Dad smiles sadly. "I remember. And I never guessed! From now on, Al, I'd like to help with his training. I only wish you'd told me about him sooner."

"I—I thought you mightn't like him."

He looks up at me. "Al," he says, "I'm not really such a bad guy as you seem to think." Carefully, the way he touched Sugar, he pats my rein hand.

Grandma turns up on Lucky's other side. "My heavens," she cries cheerfully, "Sugar Baby did well! If I was a judge he'd win! But isn't it wonderful about Jan?"

I stare down at her. She explains. "Jan O'Neal won the five hundred dollars. That's wonderful for him, you know." Grandma beams.

It would have been wonderful for me, too.

"We're heading to the barbecue," says Dad.

"You better get this fellow home to bed." He means Sugar.

I could use some bed myself, right now. I could also use some barbecue, but that's okay. Pets and livestock have to be cared for first.

"We'll see you at home." Grandma smiles at Jinny and turns away.

Dad tells Jinny, "Good try, Jane," and follows Grandma. He's never got Jinny's name right yet.

"Your dad's right," Jinny says cheerfully. "We gave it a darned good try! Come on, let's get these ponies home."

She leans forward and speaks in Jet's ear. Jet nods, twitches his poor, tight tail and turns toward home.

Lucky follows Jet on her own, by habit. Sugar Baby strains back on his rope, slowing us down. But we can't hurry through the dispersing crowd, anyhow. People pause to say "Nice try," and admire Sugar. Some of them actually say how nice it was that Jan O'Neal won. Why is everyone so pleased about that? At last we are almost through the crowd. Now there's room, Jinny reins Jet back beside us. "Look," she mutters.

Up ahead, Rowan Rich rides away.

Her head is high, her back straight. She sways gracefully to Shah's graceful pace. Even so, a cloud of dark disappointment hangs around her, so thick I can almost see it. Maybe I wouldn't notice it if I didn't move in the same dark cloud myself.

The princess won second prize—that's something. But she wanted to win the five hundred as badly as I did.

Jinny chuckles. "I bet that Tom Granger's sorry he changed sides!"

Tom stands square in the road, his clown costume bunched in his arms, looking after Rowan.

"Hey, Tom!" Jinny shouts. She kicks Jet and trots ahead to rattle Tom.

Lucky wants to follow, but I rein her back. Neither Sugar nor I have the heart to fast-forward.

* * * * * * * * * * * * **15**

*H*arry says, "I didn't know if you would come."

He smiles up at me from the cool, windy shadow of the big maple. He sits cross-legged under the tree house.

Dan lolls beside him, panting gently.

I remind him, "You gave the signal. The blue scarf on the apple branch." With a scrawled note—"4 P.M."—pinned to it.

"But you had to be pretty tough to come."

Actually, I almost didn't come.

I saw the blue scarf on the branch this morning, and I argued with myself all day. Harry won the circus. Harry tore that five hundred dollars right out of my hands. Jinny's and my hands. Why should I go meet him? So what if he hung out a blue scarf, like we agreed? I didn't have to go. I wouldn't go.

Now here I sit on Lucky under the big maple, and look down on Harry and Dan in the shade.

Harry pats the moss beside him.

I slide down Lucky, hang her bridle on a branch, and join him.

Lucky moves right off, nose to grass, tail swishing flies. Free beside her, Sugar flicks his little cotton tail and grazes.

I ask Harry, "Why aren't we in the tree house? Did the floor finally cave in?"

"Just too small," he says. "We've grown that much. It's just too small now for the both of us."

"Well, Harry Barns, I came. I'm here. So what do you want?"

Dan perks his one ear and growls at my tone.

Harry rests an arm around Dan's shoulders. "For one thing, I want a new tape recorder."

Blastoff! Staring at Harry, I see the tape recorder smashed on the road, its innards rolling around under Lucky's hoofs. "Smile!" Jinny hissed, and I smiled and bowed and forgot all about the tape recorder. Never thought of it again. Never even went to clean it up.

"Honolulu, Harry! I forgot all about it!"

"What I thought."

"I'll get you a new one." There goes my next two days' baby-sitting money.

"Well, you know, I'm rich. How about you get me half a tape recorder? On sale."

"I'll get you a whole new one."

"Half," Harry says gallantly. Firmly.

"Okay." I swallow pride and embarrassment.

"Another thing. I wanted to tell you how much it meant to me, winning that circus. So you won't be mad."

"Five hundred dollars would mean a lot to anybody. You know, if I won, I was going to—"

"Dan's my dog now. He lives at our house. He sleeps on my bed. I can buy all the dog food he'll need for years."

I lean to look into Harry's happy, brown eyes. "Good. I'm glad of that." Blastoff! To my surprise, I really am almost glad. Certainly, if

I had to lose, I would rather lose to Harry than to anybody else.

"And I bought Jan a Walkman, out of my share."

"Ha! So that's where he got it!" Jan's been weaving and wavering about worse than usual, with his ears full of music.

"You know," I tell Harry, "my folks were thrilled that Jan won that circus. Isn't that weird? I thought they were on my side."

"Oh, rotted socks! They are on your side. But they know you didn't need to win like Jan did."

"What do you mean by that?"

"You're strong, Al. You wouldn't be here now with me if you weren't strong like a . . . a . . ."

"My dad calls me an ironweed."

"A what?"

"Those tall wild flowers that always come back. He loves ironweeds because they're tough."

Harry laughs. "You've got a good dad, Al. I bet he didn't even mind about Sugar."

"No, he didn't. He loves Sugar." Almost the way I used to, myself. "He wants to help me train Sugar. He didn't even mind about Hex."

"Who the heck is Hex?"

"The black kitten Grandma couldn't give away. Dad really wanted that kitten gone. But now Hex sits in his lap and purrs."

Harry murmurs, "Look out who's coming."

Away out on Old Pasture, over blowing clover and daisies, Jinny comes riding. Wind lifts her loose red hair and Jet's black mane.

I murmur, "Maybe she hasn't seen us."

Lucky raises her head and whinnies to Jet.

"Rotted socks!" Harry whispers. "She sees us now."

Jet trumpets joyfully and breaks into a gallop.

"Well, Al," says Harry, "what about it?" He takes my hand.

"What about what?"

"Shall we let Jinny know about us?"

"About us?"

"That we're friends. Do you mind if people know?"

Harry's rough hand warms mine. I say, "I thought you didn't want them knowing, Harry."

"It's weird, but I don't mind now."

"I don't mind now, either."

Jet gallops right up to us under the maple.

Jinny folds her skinny arms and grins down at us. "So here you are! I see you found the old tree house." Jinny squints up at its dark bulk in the maple.

"Oh. So you knew about the tree house." I'm disappointed. Harry and I each thought it was our own private secret, at first. Then it was our secret together. And now . . .

"There's not much on O'Neal's Hill I don't know! My grandpa built that tree house."

Wouldn't you know!

"So, Al. Are we riding?"

Lucky trots up to Jet and nuzzles his neck, asking the same question. Sugar throws his head high and prances, but not too close to Dan. Sugar remembers how Dan used to hunt him.

"You go on," Harry tells me. And winks. His rough, warm hand squeezes mine, before it draws away.

Jinny and I canter across Old Pasture toward Rocky Rise. Wind blows hair, manes, tails, and clover. Sugar bounds in circles around us, flicking his little tail.

This is the first real riding I've done since July Fourth. I didn't go near my dumb ponies except to water them, till I saw Harry's blue scarf in the apple tree.

Then I got a carrot and called Lucky. She came to me fast and let me bridle her and climb aboard with no argument. Maybe all that silly programming we did was some good, after all.

Cantering now into the wind, I feel as if a black cloud is blowing away behind me.

At the foot of Rocky Rise we draw rein. The eager ponies paw and blow.

Jinny turns to me. "You look like you finally got over that circus."

"Maybe I have."

"You know what, you took it too serious."

"I had such big plans!"

"Oh, right. You wanted to buy a saddle."

"And the Arabian."

"Huh?" Jinny darts me a grin. Then she sobers. "You meant that? You really, actually wanted an Arabian horse?"

"In the worst way," I admit.

"Honolulu, Al! You weren't actually going to sell your miracle ponies!"

"Actually, I was. You know, now I can't believe it."

Lucky shifts and shakes her head. She knows the next thing we do is race up Rocky Rise, and she wants a head start. Sugar bounds high, long legs stiff. Jet paws and whinnies to Jinny to loosen rein.

Wind blows away the last of my black cloud.

Our ponies are lively and fun. Their warm coats glow in late sunshine. Sugar knows me. Lucky trusts me. She is my miracle, rainbow pony.

Inside, I feel a rainbow glow, and arc, and spread. I haven't felt that in a while. I haven't felt it since winning five hundred dollars came to mean the world to me, and a dream horse seemed more important than my real live miracle ponies themselves.

I tell Jinny, "Actually, I must have been coconuts."

"Bingo," Jinny agrees. "Affirmative in the extreme! Race you up the Rise, Al. Yaaah, Jet!"

"Yaaah, Lucky!"

I only need to let the reins loose. Lucky shoots like a rocket up Rocky Rise. Jet pounds beside us. Sugar darts ahead.